By Michael Pryor

Illustrated by Daron Parton

Pearson Australia
(a division of Pearson Australia Group Pty Ltd)
707 Collins Street, Melbourne, Victoria 3008
PO Box 23360, Melbourne, Victoria 8012
www.pearson.com.au

First published 2010 by Pearson Australia
2019 2018 2017 2016
10 9 8 7 6 5 4 3 2

Publisher: Simone Calderwood
Illustrator: Daron Parton
Editor: Anne McKenna
Designer: Glen McClay
Copyright & Pictures Editor: Caitlin O'Brien
Project Editor: Aisling Coughlan
Production Controller: Claire Henry
Printed in Australia by the SOS Print + Media Group

ISBN 978 1 4425 2441 5

Pearson Australia Group Pty Ltd ABN 40 004 245 943

CONTENTS

Chapter 1

THE BRAIN WAVE

"Marco!" Phil yelled.

I stopped hammering. "What?"

"I don't think I can hold this branch back for much longer!"

"Why not?"

"There's a spider on it."

This was serious. Phil had a problem with spiders. He was the sort who could never go to sleep in a room once he saw a spider in it.

"Look, Phil, you can't let go now! I've nearly finished!"

Nailing a flagpole to the top of the tree house had been Phil's idea in the first place. It was typical, though, how I was the one who ended up doing the most dangerous work. I took a deep breath. We were up pretty high. I could see the council offices and the library from up here.

"It's a big spider, Marco."

"Phil! Don't you let go of that branch! I'm warning you!"

I was about to tell him what I'd do if he let go—when he let go.

Some time later, I was lying on the springy grass at the base of the tree in Phil's backyard. I was looking up at the sky and it was nice and restful. It was blue, and the clouds were like chocolate snowballs with all the chocolate picked off.

When I went to scratch my nose, I found that I had something heavy in my hand. It didn't look like it would be good for scratching noses. It was a hammer.

A face loomed into view. It was Phil. I shuddered.

"Are you okay, Marco?" He rubbed his hands together and looked eager. "And if you aren't, can I do First Aid?"

"Don't touch me." I staggered to my feet and dusted myself off. I glared at him. "A spider, hey?"

"Well, I thought it was a spider…"

"You thought it was a spider."

"It was really a leaf."

"Right," I said. "So I got knocked out of a tree and nearly broke my neck because you were scared of a leaf? This is a great way to start the school holidays."

Phil looked hurt. "It could have been a poisonous leaf. You know, with fangs and claws and stuff like that."

I sighed. Phil was my next-door neighbour. We'd been friends ever since we were in nappies. We grew up throwing sand at each other in the sandpit. As we got older, I found out that Phil had a knack for stupid projects. Like nailing a flagpole to the top of the tree house.

Phil's projects usually came about when he was bored. That's when he started having ideas.

But best friends are hard to find. So despite all of Phil's annoying, irritating and dangerous habits, I stuck with him. And Phil stuck with me, for some reason or other. Whatever else he was, he was definitely loyal.

"Look, Phil," I said, after I'd made sure that I had no broken bones. I found plenty of bruises, but I could cope with them. If you were a friend of Phil, you had to expect a few bruises. "Is this flagpole such a good idea?" I nudged it with my foot.

Phil crossed his arms and looked determined. "Marco. I didn't say it'd be easy."

"Yes, you did."

He shrugged. "That doesn't matter. This is a tough job, a dangerous job, a difficult job."

"You didn't say that, either. 'A pushover' was what you said, if I remember correctly."

He waved that away. "But when the going gets tough, the going gets going." He blinked. "Or something like that."

"Phil, did that branch hit you on the head?"

"Nope. I ducked." He held up a finger. "Marco, if we don't get that flagpole up on our tree house, Dean Green will go around telling everyone that his tree house is the best."

I thought about that for a moment. "It is the best."

"Only because he got his dad to help! They used a crane! His tree house even has glass in the windows!"

"Well, we would have had a flagpole if you hadn't let go of that branch." I nudged the flagpole again, then I stared at it. "Phil. We don't have a flag. Why were we putting up a flagpole?"

Phil looked blank. Then he scratched his head. "Good point. Maybe we should have started with a flag." He smiled. "Come on. Let's get something to eat."

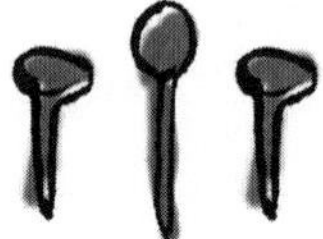

Eating was Phil's answer to most things.
A problem? Think about it over a sandwich.
A successful practical joke? Congratulate yourself with a mango.

When we reached Phil's house, Digger trotted around the corner and barked. It was his "Where have you been?" bark. He looked offended that we hadn't included him in our tree house adventure. Then he turned tail and disappeared around the corner of the house.

"Where's he going?" I asked.

"He might have just remembered an appointment," Phil said. "To see a dog about a man."

"What?"

"Never mind. Ah, there's a good dog!"

Digger appeared again. This time, he had a newspaper in his mouth. He dropped it at Phil's feet and gave his "Aren't I clever?" bark.

"I love the local paper," Phil said, as he patted Digger on the head. "It's interesting."

"Sure it is," I said. "I wonder what's on the front page this week? A big picture of a cat stuck up a tree? A street sign that fell over?"

"I always wanted my picture on the front page of the paper," Phil said, dreamily. He picked it up. "It's a bit soggy. Dog spit."

He unrolled the paper. Then his eyes went wide. His face went pale. His jaw hung open. "No! It can't be!"

"What?"

"Dean Green. It's him. On the front page of the newspaper."

"Really? He's been arrested for something?"

Phil shuddered. "No. He's some sort of hero."

I took the paper from Phil's hands. He hardly moved.

I stared at the big photo of Dean Green on the front of *The Glenbrae Reporter*. He was standing outside the Glenbrae Library, right in front of the columns. He was shaking hands with a man so old, shrivelled and bent up that he looked like a walking Twistie.

"I can't stand it," Phil groaned. "Dean Green, local hero."

The Glenbrae
Reporter
LIBRARY
Local hero
Dean Green
e jobs for local firm
TDOOR
NITURE
DENTAL
SELF
STORAGE

"I bet he didn't do any of this stuff by himself," I said. "See what it says here: 'Dean Green, with the help of his mother, has interviewed Glenbrae's oldest citizen, 98-year-old Cyril Judkins, about town history—and found out more about famous bushranger Captain Frightful. Cyril's father was an eyewitness when Captain Frightful baled up the mail coach loaded with gold. Dean's interview will be aired on local radio this weekend.'"

"Gaah! Front page of the paper *and* he's on the radio! It's awful!"

"We should be on the front of the paper instead of Dean Green," I said.

Phil grabbed my arm, hard. He stared at me, then he shook a fist in the air. "Yes! You're right, Marco!"

"I'm right?"

"You bet. We deserve to be on the front page instead of Dean Green—and we can do it, all by ourselves! It's our dream!"

"Your dream."

Phil glanced at me. "I'm happy to share."

Then he shook his fist in the air again. "It's our dream, our hope, our destiny!"

I sighed. I knew that once Phil got wound up like this, it was impossible to stop him. All I could do was hang on for the ride.

"I see that we have a mission," I said.

"That's right," Phil said. "Project Front Page has just begun."

Chapter 2

UNBALANCED

The next day, I'd forgotten all about Project Front Page. Over breakfast, I was thinking about why bananas were curved. Why weren't apples curved, or oranges? Would they taste different if they were?

I ate my cereal slowly while I thought this over. When Phil's face appeared at the kitchen window, I nearly choked.

"Phil! What are you doing here? And what's that on your head?"

He grinned and waved very slowly. "Come out here and I'll show you how we're getting on the front page of the newspaper."

Phil's projects were funny things. Most of them were like dead-end streets—they didn't go anywhere. But some were stubborn. They stuck around and before you knew it, you were involved in something that was likely to end up in humiliation. At best.

Outside, I stared at him. "Phil, I might be going crazy, but it looks like you've got three dinner plates stuck on your head."

"They're not stuck." He beamed at me—without moving his head. "I'm balancing them. And I've got more in that box over there."

"Okay. It might be a stupid question, but why are you balancing plates on your head?"

"Project Front Page," he said. "The best way to get your picture in the paper is to break a world record. Plate balancing is perfect! It makes a great photo and how hard can it be? I've just started this morning and I'm already up to three."

"And you want me to do this, too?"

"Of course! We're a team! Watch how easy it is!"

Phil held out both hands, then spread his arms wide. He marched slowly, like a tight-rope walker. The plates wobbled a little, but he tilted his head slightly and steadied them.

"Not bad," I said. Then I frowned. "Those plates look funny."

"Funny? How?"

"Well, they don't look like your mum's best china, for a start."

"I should hope not." Phil started to shudder, but stopped as the plates on his head shook. "They're plastic. You know, just starting out, I didn't want to risk the dinner set."

"Good thinking."

Phil reached the back fence, then turned and walked back. His arms were outstretched, his pace was slow and deliberate.

Digger stared at him and gave his "I don't believe my eyes" bark.

"See? It's a snap. Now it's your turn." Phil plucked the plates from his head and held them out.

"Three plates?" I snorted. "Is that the best you can do? I think I can do better than three lousy plates. Give me some more."

"Don't be stupid, Marco. I've been practising all morning. You're just starting."

"Hand 'em over. I think I'm a natural at plate balancing."

It was a challenge. Phil couldn't resist. "Stand back, Marco. First of all, you have to watch an expert at work. Look and learn, my friend, look and learn."

Phil marched to a box on the step next to the rubbish bins. He peered in. "Let me see. Blue's my favourite colour, so I'll have a blue one. And a red one too, and that yellow one looks good. And the three I started with makes six. But seven's my lucky number, so I'd better have that white one as well."

"Phil, that's a lot of plates."

"Stand back and watch the master."

One by one, Phil stacked all seven plates on his head.

He held them for a moment, then he let go.

At first, he just stood still. The plates wobbled, then shifted, then they settled down. "See? Nothing to it."

"Okay, genius," I said. "Let's see you walk to the fence."

"Easy."

He took one slow step, then a second. The plates stayed firmly on his head. He took one more step, then another.

"Come on!" I called, even though I was impressed. "You're walking like a robot. Loosen up a bit."

Phil took two quick steps, then a few more. But as he moved faster, the plates began to tilt. Soon he was tottering, trying to stop the plates from falling off. He started zigzagging across the yard, doing his best to keep the plates upright. But the faster he went, the more the plates started overbalancing.

"Uh-oh," I said.

"I'm okay!" Phil cried, as he lurched forward. The plates trembled on the edge of falling off. He kept looking up, trying to watch the plates. "I've got 'em."

“Watch out for Digger!”

Digger was lying in the sun, asleep on his back with all four paws in the air. Phil saw him at the last minute and took a giant step right over him. The plates swayed and tilted. Phil leaned to his right, then back to his left. He jerked his head back a little, and then began staggering forward again, plates still on top of his head.

"Phil! Look out for the rubbish bins!"

"Don't worry! I'm fine!"

"Phil! Look out for the sandpit!"

"It's okay! I'm steady as a rock!"

"Phil! Look out for the fish pond!"

"So I'm a bit wet! What's the problem?"

"Phil! Look out for the in-ground trampoline!"

"Look out for the what?"

BOOOOOOOOOING!

I looked over the back fence. Phil was sprawled on the compost heap. The plates had disappeared. He had grass clippings in his hair, a tomato skin on one ear and a cabbage leaf on his nose.

"Compost," I said.

"Looks like it." Phil sniffed. He picked the cabbage leaf off his nose and threw it away. "Smells like it, too. Hmm. I have an idea."

"Forget plate balancing?"

"The world record is ninety-two plates."

"Okay. Forget plate balancing. What's Project Front Page Stage Two?"

"We're going to grow an unusual vegetable."

Chapter 3

BIG VEGGIES

The next day, I went to Phil's house. He took me out the back and pointed to where a wheelbarrow, a shovel and a pick were waiting.

"This is the place for our veggie patch," he said, proudly. "Whopping big vegetables or vegetables in weird shapes always get in the paper!"

I stared. This corner of Phil's backyard was like the surface of the moon. Bare, dry and cracked, it looked like nothing had ever grown there.

"We've got a lot of hard work to do," I said.

"True, but the price of fame is hard work."

"And the price of hard work is blisters, I reckon," I said. "Okay, so this is our veggie patch. I know what we're going to grow."

"So do I."

"A giant pumpkin. Big pumpkins always get in the paper."

Phil made a face. "I hate pumpkin. I think we should grow the world's biggest watermelon."

"Watermelon's disgusting. I think we should try broad beans."

"Carrots."

"Zucchini."

"Brussels sprouts."

"You've got to be joking. Tomatoes."

"Celery."

"Kohl rabi."

Phil stared. "You just made that up!"

"I didn't. It's like a purple turnip."

Phil shook his head. "We're never going to decide."

"Let's try Rock, Paper, Scissors."

"Okay," Phil said. "But no Dynamite, Uncuttable Paper or 'Can't Break 'em' Scissors. Just ordinary Rock, Paper, Scissors."

"Best of three?"

"Nope. One go, and that's it."

I thought hard. Phil usually played safe and went for the middle—scissors. So I should choose rock. But Phil would know that I knew that, so he'd choose paper. Which meant that I should choose paper...

My head started to hurt.

"Ready?" Phil said. "One, two, THREE!"

We thrust out our hands. I sighed. "Rock versus paper. You win, Phil."

"I always win. Why don't you get used to it?" Phil tapped his chin thoughtfully. "Now, I do believe we should try to grow a watermelon."

"Watermelon!"

"No complaining. Remember, I am the Lord of Rock, Paper, Scissors. Now, let's dig up this veggie patch."

"Stand back." I took the pick. "I'll make a start."

I swung the pick at the bare earth and I thought someone had rung a huge bell. The pick struck hard and bounced off. My whole body shook. Tiny, hard splinters of earth flew into the air.

"Ow!" Phil said. "Watch it!"

I dropped the pick and wrung my hands. "I must have hit a rock."

I moved a metre or so to the left and swung again. More pain, more splinters.

"Another rock?" Phil frowned. "Try over there."

I gave up after ten swings. My whole body was aching. "Are you growing rocks here or something?"

Phil took the shovel and jabbed at the earth. He didn't make a mark. "It's hard, but I don't think it's rocky. Look, it's just baked, hard dirt." He shook his head. "We're not going to get far with this."

I had to agree, but it was disappointing. Then I saw the hose.

"Look," I said, after I turned it on and dragged it over. "We leave this running for a few hours and it'll be nice and soft."

"Great idea, genius," Phil said. He took a step back when the water nearly splashed his feet. "But Project Front Page doesn't wait. If we're going to get our picture in the paper, we need to go to Stage Three."

I nodded. "I agree. Stage Three. Excellent. Can't wait."

"You have no idea what Stage Three is, do you?"

"Nope. What is it?"

"Project Front Page Stage Three is where we really put this town on the map. Follow me."

Chapter 4

FRIGHTFUL TOWN?

"And what exactly is Stage Three again?" I asked.

Phil had led the way to the Glenbrae Library, past the columns, up the stairs and into the foyer. He pointed at the big oil painting over the main doors. "Look up there."

"Captain Frightful holds up the mail coach." I shrugged. "So? It's the only interesting thing that's ever happened in this town. Dean Green got in the paper and on the radio because of it."

Captain Frightful was one of the worst bushrangers in history. He held up the mail coach on the road that now runs right through Glenbrae, then he immediately got lost in the bush with a sack full of letters. When the police found him, he'd burned most of them to keep warm.

"This town loves Captain Frightful," said Phil.

"True." We used to have a gift shop in the main street, right next to the post office. It sold Captain Frightful tea towels and Captain Frightful mugs and Captain Frightful T-shirts with the world's lamest slogan on it: "Captain Frightful, He's Delightful!"

No wonder the gift shop went broke.

But Glenbrae did love our failure of a bushranger. There was another painting of him in the council offices, and every so often there was a movement to rename Glenbrae as "Frightful Town". He may have been a failure of a bushranger, but he was our bushranger.

"If we do something about him," Phil said, "we'll be heroes, featured on the front page, and someone's bound to start a web page or two about us. About him, I mean."

"Okay, so that's Project Front Page Stage Three."

"It only gets better. Listen. We're going to make a local tourist attraction."

We had a tourist once in Glenbrae. I think she was lost. "A tourist attraction," I repeated.

"A tourist attraction to beat all tourist attractions." He took a deep breath "We're going to make a life-sized animated model of the hold-up of the mail coach, complete with lights and everything." He beamed. "It's called a diorama. We'll become instant celebrities."

"Instant idiots, more like it."

“I can see it now.” His eyes were bright. “Captain Frightful on his horse, waving his pistols. The mail coach with terrified passengers. Guards throwing down their guns. Beards everywhere.”

“Agreed. Got to have lots of beards whenever there’s a bushranger.”

Phil thrust a finger at me. “Marco, Project Front Page cannot fail!”

Chapter 5

WILD MAN RAYMOND

Later that afternoon, we were peering through a tall wire fence.

"You see anyone?" Phil asked, anxiously.

"No. I'm not sure about this." I wrinkled my nose at the smell that drifted through the fence.

"Look, Marco. If we're going to make a good display, we need good materials. Do you have lots of money stashed away somewhere?"

"No."

"Neither do I. So we can't buy good materials. We'll have to use recycled materials."

"You mean stuff other people have thrown away."

"That's right. And that's why we're at the tip."

"But what about Wild Man Raymond?"

"You saw the garbage truck go out," Phil said. "He won't be back for ages."

Wild Man Raymond lived at the tip and he was a local legend among the kids. I'd never actually seen him, but I knew that Wild Man Raymond was about two metres tall, with a long straggly beard, red-rimmed eyes, and fingernails that could cut steel. He hated brave and clever kids who tried to take stuff from the tip. And he had a dog.

Not just any dog. Brutus was as big as a lion, and liked to snack on car tyres and old concrete. At least, that's what Phil told me. Anyone found inside the tip fence was fair game for Brutus.

"Okay," I said. My palms were sweating. My heart had started thumping like a drum. "Let's be quick."

"This way. Around the back."

Phil led the way to where part of the tip fence had fallen over. We carefully squeezed through the wire and then scrambled past some trees and bushes.

"Look at that," Phil whispered. He pointed at Wild Man Raymond's house. "It's a treasure trove."

The house was small but surprisingly neat. It was painted a cheery yellow and it had striped sun-blinds over the windows. Behind the house was a large yard, full of stuff plucked from the tip. And it was all arranged with care.

Piles of timber were stacked against a wooden fence, all organised by length and thickness. Next to these stacks were dozens of old car bodies, red with rust. These were lined up according to size, biggest to smallest. Thousands of bottles had been set up in pyramids taller than I was.

A row of battered lawn mowers stood in front of dozens of TV sets, most of which had no tube. They looked like eyeless monsters. Big piles of assorted junk were kept in large wooden bins against one fence.

I couldn't believe the stuff people had just thrown away. "Look! Is that an aeroplane?"

"Just half," Phil said. He shook his head, wide-eyed at all these goodies. It was Phil's idea of heaven—lots of stuff that could be turned into other stuff with a bit of imagination. "This has to be the neatest tip in the world."

I looked at Phil. "Are we allowed to just take this?"

"Wild Man Raymond lets people come and sort through it once a month. We just need it now, that's all, and his next open day is three weeks away. So we're just getting in ahead of time." He rubbed his chin thoughtfully. "Besides, we're recycling. It's good for the dolphins."

"Dolphins?"

"Whatever."

Nervously, I followed Phil as he pushed out of the bushes. I felt exposed as we crossed the hard ground to the yard. We scrambled over the wooden fence and Phil ran to the nearest bin of assorted rubbish.

"Ah!" he said and he rubbed his hands together. "Perfect—a bicycle horn!"

"What's that for?"

"The mail coach. It'll look good."

The bicycle horn was on top of a pile of brass taps and ornaments. Phil leaned over and gently plucked it as if he were picking an apple.

Immediately, a siren went off on top of Wild Man Raymond's house.

It was the loudest thing I'd ever heard. It felt like someone was hitting both of my ears with hammers. "You've done it now!" I shouted at Phil. I was sure that Wild Man Raymond had some sort of Tip Intruder Detection System monitoring every single piece of junk in the tip. I had visions of a bank of computer screens inside his house, and some sort of computer intelligence that was zeroing in on us with a high-powered laser RIGHT NOW. "Put it back! Let's get out of here!"

Suddenly, the siren stopped and the yard was filled with a creepy silence. "See?" Phil grinned. "There's nothing to worry about. Now, what's next?"

I didn't say anything. My ears were still ringing from the noise of the siren, for a start, but mostly it was because whenever Phil said "There's nothing to worry about", I got very, very worried.

Then, in the distance, from the far corner of the tip, I heard the sound of howling. It was wild and terrifying, which was bad enough, but at that moment I was sure that it sounded hungry, which was worse. "Brutus," I whispered and all the sweat on my body suddenly went cold.

"What?" Phil was still poking about in the pile of brass.

I grabbed his arm and jerked him upright. I shook him by the shoulders.

"It's Brutus! Wild Man Raymond's dog! He mustn't have gone on the truck. We've got to get out of here!"

Phil went pale. "But we need some of this stuff! Project Front Page Stage Three depends on it!"

I looked around and grabbed an old pram. "Quick. Fill this up."

Desperately, I pushed the pram around the piles of rubbish while Phil hurled junk into it.

"Hurry!" I said, as the howling grew louder. "He's getting closer!"

"Done! Let's go!"

We used the pram as a battering ram and burst through a rotten part of the fence. Splinters flew, but I didn't care. We had to get out of there. Together, we dragged the pram back through the tip, past the trees and bushes, and over to the fallen-down wire fence, faster than that pram had ever travelled before.

When we finally wrestled the pram over the fence, I took the chance to look back. "I can see him!"

Brutus wasn't quite as big as a lion, but he was the largest dog I'd ever seen. He looked like he was part Rottweiler, part bulldog and part monster.

The only things small about him were his eyes, which were little and piggy. He was black and grey. His great mouth was wide open, and I could see his teeth. He was bounding towards us, weaving through the piles of junk, the earth thundering beneath his mighty feet.

Phil turned, saw my staring eyes and he looked in the same direction.

"Waaaargh!" he cried.

"Waaaargh!" I agreed.

Words didn't really seem good enough to describe the terror that had taken hold of me.

A scream did the trick nicely, though, I found.

We looked at each other. Phil looked just as terrified as I felt.

Still shrieking, we both grabbed the handle of the pram. In a split second, we were off as if we were rocket-powered, leaving a cloud of dust behind us. We wove down the track, barely dodging the trees that lined the gravel way, still shrieking. It seemed to help.

After some time of this warp-speed pram travel, we slowed down. We had to. No human body could keep that up.

Phil dropped the handle of the pram and let it coast to a stop at the base of a gum tree. He bent over double and put his hands on his knees.

"I think—" He stopped and panted for a moment. "I think we've left him behind."

My legs were like rubber. I put my hands on my hips and sucked in huge breaths of air. "I don't care. I won't be happy until we're well away from this place."

We trudged on, ignoring any puzzled stares as we got into town.

"Short cut here," Phil wheezed and pointed. "Through the playground and over our back fence."

Our feet were dragging as we pushed the pram past the seesaw, past the slide, past the monkey bars. Eventually, we reached the fence and parked the pram. My heart was still hammering, but it was starting to slow down. "That was close."

Phil wiped his face with his hands. Then he grinned. "See? There's nothing to worry about."

I groaned. "Don't say that."

"Why not?"

"Because things go wrong whenever you say that."

"Like what?"

A low growl came from behind us. It was deep, gruff and still hungry. Slowly, I turned around. "Like that."

Brutus was standing on the far side of the playground. He didn't look happy at having to follow us right through town, although I had trouble imagining him ever looking happy.

He snapped his jaws together and it sounded like a steel trap.

"Waaaargh!" I said.

"Waaaargh!" Phil agreed.

We threw ourselves at the fence, launched ourselves over it—and landed in knee-deep mud.

"Waaaargh!" I said again.

"We forgot to turn off the hose!"

We'd landed face down in what was going to be the veggie patch. The hose we'd left running had turned the whole backyard into an expanse of black, evil-smelling mud.

Phil lifted his head. The mud dripped off him in thick, gluey globs. He struggled to his feet and wiped his face. It only made it worse. "You look awful," he said.

"Thanks." I sat up. I shook my head and bits of mud spattered Phil. "Let's forget the veggie-growing idea, okay?"

"Okay." Phil went to the fence and peered over. I joined him.

Brutus had gone. The pram had gone. All that was left were some wheels.

"What happened?" Phil said.

"I think Brutus ate the pram."

"Oh."

Then I saw a truck rumbling up the street away from us. It was Wild Man Raymond's tip truck, but I didn't tell Phil. I wanted Phil to be horrified by Brutus the pram-eating dog, so he'd never suggest a little trip to the tip again.

We went to the front yard. I found the hose and sprayed Phil until he was clean. Then he did the same for me. Digger stared at us and gave his "You guys are crazy" bark.

"What's that in your letterbox?" I asked, as I wiped water from my eyes.

Phil trotted over and grabbed the pink piece of paper. "Hard rubbish removal tomorrow," he read. "Leave out all unwanted furniture, building materials and junk."

I sighed. "So we didn't have to risk our lives at the tip?"

"Nope. We can just wander along the footpath and look at what people want to throw out." He brightened. "Project Front Page still lives!"

Chapter 6

MAKE A MODEL!

Four days of hard work later, we finished the mail coach.

It was hot in Phil's garage as we admired our work. I was sitting down on a rusty clothes dryer, wiping the sweat from my forehead. Phil had collapsed on a pile of old carpet squares.

"It's beautiful," he said.

"Majestic," I agreed. I had to. It was true.

Most of the mail coach had once been a giant cardboard box for a refrigerator. I'd found some brown paint and Phil had sawn out the windows.

We'd done some Googling and printed off some images we were using as a guide, to make sure we had it all perfect. We'd glued on other cardboard boxes for the driver's seat and the lumpy bit at the back. I wasn't quite sure what that bit was, and neither was Phil, but we knew it had to be there. The whole thing balanced on four old pram wheels that looked suspiciously like the wheels from our record-breaking speedy pram.

The mail coach wasn't life-sized. Early on, we agreed that was too ambitious. But it was nearly as tall as I was, and we both thought it was a pretty good start. I was already seeing it all lit up, with computer-controlled doors opening and closing—it was going to be great.

"Right," Phil said. "Now, the rest." He rubbed his hands together. "What's missing, Marco?"

"Well, horses, for a start. A mail coach needs horses. Captain Frightful needs a horse. Where are we going to get horses?"

Phil leapt to his feet, grinning. "I hoped you'd ask that. I've been keeping this for a surprise."

He rushed out of the garage. I could hear him out the back, throwing things around. Finally, he staggered back into the garage with something large, fuzzy and red in his arms.

I slowly got to my feet and stared.

Phil put it down and patted it proudly. “It’s a reindeer.” He reached over and snapped off the fuzzy red antlers. “Now it’s a horse.”

I stared some more. The reindeer was chest-high, and as well as being red and fuzzy, it was covered with gold braid. “Where did you get it?”

“McGinty’s Newsagency threw out ten of these. I rescued them.”

I slowly approached the reindeer-horse and patted it. Then I looked at Phil with some awe. “This is beautiful. I think we’re going to have some fun with Captain Frightful.”

Chapter 7

COACH OF THE YEAR

It took another week, but finally we were done.

Captain Frightful sat on his noble horse, threatening the terrified driver and passengers in their sturdy mail coach. At least, that was what it was meant to look like.

A shop dummy with a big floppy hat sat on a reindeer that had its antlers broken off. The dummy was wearing a giant overcoat that almost reached the ground. It looked as if a small furry terrier was attacking its face.

"Nice beard on Captain Frightful," I said, as we gazed proudly at our work.

"Thanks," Phil said. "It was actually one of Aunt Julia's wigs. She'll never know it's missing."

"Good pistol, too. Doesn't look like it used to be a hair dryer. At least, not from a distance."

I had to admit the mail coach was impressive. Its brown sides and mysterious boxes made it very convincing. The four reindeer-horses pulling it still looked a bit Christmassy, especially with the tinsel, but I decided you couldn't have everything.

The driver of the mail coach was a giant-sized teddy bear in a rubber raincoat. He had a floppy hat on, too. His beard was cotton wool that Phil had painted black and stuck all over his face.

The passengers inside the mail coach were a mixed bunch. There were a couple of blow-up dinosaurs, a scarecrow, two big rag dolls and a plastic glow-in-the-dark skeleton.

"All sorts of people came to the goldfields," I pointed out. "From all over the world."

Phil rubbed his hands together. "Now, let's test that driver's assistant one more time."

This was the best part, and we'd spent ages on it. The driver's assistant was a dressmaker's dummy on a stick. It had the usual floppy hat, big coat and scruffy beard.

Phil had painted a terrified expression on the dummy, with a wide-open mouth and staring eyes. The stick was attached to a motor that I'd taken out of a wrecked washing machine.

Phil had cut a little hatch in the top of the mail coach. When the motor was turned on, the driver's assistant would pop up, look terrified at seeing Captain Frightful, then pop back down again. The idea was that this would go on, over and over, to add some action to the scene.

"Okay," I said, and I flipped the switch.

The mail coach rattled. The washing machine motor went chugga-chugga-chugga. The passengers and the driver shook. Then the driver's assistant shot up through the hole, looked very scared, and dropped back down again. A few seconds later, it repeated the action. Up, scared, down again. Up, scared, down again.

"Perfect!" Phil crowed. "What a crowd pleaser!

I'll go and ring the newspaper to tell them the big opening of Glenbrae's best tourist attraction is tomorrow night."

I was tired, happy and relieved. "All the hard work is done. Now we just have to sit back and listen to the cheers."

Chapter 8

SHOW TIME!

The night was warm. The word had got around and a crowd had gathered in front of Phil's place. We stood at the picket fence and looked at the mums and dads, grans and grandads and kids of all ages.

I nudged Phil. "Look, it's Dean Green. And his mum."

Phil smiled. "He's in for a treat, then."

"He's going to be so jealous," I muttered.

Phil clapped his hands together. "Ladies and gentlemen," he announced, and the crowd hushed. "Good to see you all here. This is an important time in the history of Glenbrae." He nudged me. "Get ready to hit the switches."

I hurried over to the power board that we'd set up near the front door. I tried to remember which switch turned on what.

"Ladies and gentlemen," Phil repeated. He was enjoying himself. "We present to you, Captain Frightful's Greatest Moment."

I shrugged and flipped the first three switches. One floodlight snapped on. A second followed it, and, in the middle of the front yard, a collection of lumpy shapes was revealed.

"Oooh," went the crowd.

"Aaah," went the crowd.

"What's that?" went the crowd.

"Marco," Phil hissed. "Take the sheets off!"

We'd used some old sheets to keep our project secret. Phil was meant to whip them off, but he'd obviously been enjoying his job as Host of the Great Event too much to remember.

I snapped off the lights, scurried over, whipped the sheets off, then raced back to the power board. "This time for sure," I muttered.

"Ladies and gentlemen," Phil said, for a third time. "Captain Frightful's Greatest Moment!"

I was ready. The lights burst into life. One lit up the figure of Captain Frightful on the horse. Another lit the mail coach. The third was a tiny light inside the mail coach.

The crowd applauded, but soon laughter began to ripple through the spectators.

"Marco," Phil hissed. "The driver's assistant!"

I flipped the last switch. With a groan, the washing machine motor started. The dressmaker's dummy slowly rose, paused, looked scared, then groaned downwards. The crowd went crazy.

I hurried to join Phil. He was beaming. "We've done it! Now, where's that photographer?"

At that moment, the mail coach shuddered. The washing machine motor whined, and the driver's assistant didn't appear.

"It's stuck," I said. We'd had this problem before, but I thought I'd fixed it.

"Come on." Phil raced over and I was close behind.

While the onlookers made suggestions that they thought were funny, I put my hand on the mail coach. "It's hot," I hissed.

The cardboard shuddered.

"The washing machine's making a funny noise, too," Phil said.

"Quick, it's overloaded. We've got to free the dummy. Where's the stepladder?"

Phil propped up the stepladder and held it while I poked at the dummy with a handy screwdriver. "I think I've got it. The coat's caught," I muttered.

From the base of the ladder, Phil sniffed. "Can you smell smoke?"

Suddenly, there was a loud tearing sound. I jerked back and the ladder was immediately wobbly.

I glanced down and saw Phil's stunned face, then the ladder disappeared from beneath me.

I fell—just in time.

The driver's assistant—the dressmaker's dummy—shot upwards like a sky rocket.

It barely missed me. It screamed straight up, its beard on fire, heading for the heavens.

The crowd went silent with awe.

I landed in the lavender bush and stared at the flaming driver's assistant in the sky. Phil stood, open-mouthed, and tilted his head back to follow it. Flaming and flapping, it soared up and up, higher and higher. It grew even brighter as the hat and coat caught fire.

The silence broke. The crowd went wild.

Cheering and clapping, the good citizens of Glenbrae welcomed their new tourist attraction. A few of them even rolled on the footpath, laughing.

The flaming driver's assistant reached the top of its flight. Gracefully, high overhead, it slowed, stopped, then began to fall—still on fire.

"Uh-oh," Phil said.

I got to my feet. "Did this happen to Captain Frightful?"

"If it did, nothing on the web mentioned it."

The flaming driver's assistant tumbled down, falling back to earth, picking up speed as it went, the flames getting bigger and bigger all the time.

I couldn't move. I watched, helpless, as it crashed right onto the mail coach.

Naturally, the mail coach burst into flame. I sighed. "I'll turn off the electricity. You get the hose, Phil."

It took a while, but we finally put out the fire. The crowd, of course, stayed to watch the whole show, laughing and hooting and offering advice. The people only drifted away after Phil used the bird bath to put out the last of the flames.

The fire brigade arrived. When Phil explained what had happened, they drove off. They were all laughing, too.

Phil wiped soot from his face. I studied the wreckage of all our work. Captain Frightful was just a soggy pile of ash and melted plastic. The mail coach was a mound of ash, scorched metal and plastic. The reindeer were sad, black shapes.

"What a disaster," Phil said.

"Maybe not," I said. "Look."

A woman with a camera jumped over the gate.

"What a show!" she chuckled. "Come on you

guys, stand in front of the ruins! I want to put this on the front page of *The Glenbrae Reporter*!"

"You do?" Phil brightened.

"Sure thing. YOUNG FIREFIGHTERS SAVE THE DAY! Now, stand up straight."

Phil thumped me on the back. "We've done it. Project Front Page is a success!"

The photographer pointed at us. "Say 'Cheese'!"